PENGUIN CLASSICS

*Grave of the Fireflies*

*Grave of the Fireflies*

AKIYUKI NOSAKA

*Translated by Ginny Tapley Takemori*

PENGUIN BOOKS

PENGUIN CLASSICS

UK | USA | Canada | Ireland | Australia
India | New Zealand | South Africa

Penguin Classics is part of the Penguin Random House group of companies
whose addresses can be found at global.penguinrandomhouse.com.

Penguin Random House UK
One Embassy Gardens, 8 Viaduct Gardens, London SW11 7BW

penguin.co.uk

*Hotaru No Haka* included in *American Hijiki, Hotaru No Haka* by Akiyuki Nosaka

This translation first published in Great Britain in Penguin Classics 2025
002

Copyright © Yoko Nosaka 1968

Original Japanese edition published in 1972 by SHINCHOSHA Publishing Co., Ltd.

This English edition published by arrangement with SHINCHOSHA Publishing
Co., Ltd, In care of Tuttle-Mori Agency, Inc., Tokyo.
Translation copyright © Ginny Tapley Takemori, 2025

No part of this book may be used or reproduced in any manner for the
purpose of training artificial intelligence technologies or systems. In accordance
with Article 4(3) of the DSM Directive 2019/790, Penguin Random House
expressly reserves this work from the text and data mining exception.

The moral rights of the author and translator have been asserted

Set in Dante MT Pro 12.8/16pt
Typeset by Six Red Marbles UK, Thetford, Norfolk
Printed and bound in Great Britain by Clays Ltd, Elcograf S.p.A.

The authorized representative in the EEA is Penguin Random House Ireland,
Morrison Chambers, 32 Nassau Street, Dublin D02 YH68

A CIP catalogue record for this book is available from the British Library

ISBN: 978-0-241-78021-3

Penguin Random House is committed to a sustainable future
for our business, our readers and our planet. This book is made from
Forest Stewardship Council® certified paper.

*Grave of the Fireflies*

In the mainline Sannomiya Station, bayside exit, Seita sat slumped against a column, its tiles peeling off to expose the bare concrete, with his bottom on the floor and both legs stretched out straight before him. He was sunburned to a frazzle and hadn't washed for almost a month, yet his emaciated cheeks were sunken and pale. Come nightfall, he gazed at the silhouettes of men talking rowdily with excessive bravado as they warmed themselves around the watch fire like bandits. In the morning he saw children his age heading off to middle school as if nothing were amiss, distinguishing between the khaki-clad boys with white bundles from the top prefectural school and those with satchels on their backs from the city school, and girls sporting sailor tops over their baggy wartime pantaloons, the folds of their collars indicating whether they attended the prestigious prefectural school or one of the three expensive private academies. The legs of the crowds filed purposefully past, either taking no notice or jumping to avoid him, as people looked down alerted by his stench. But Seita no longer had the strength to crawl to the nearby toilet.

War orphans clustered around the base of each of the solid metre-thick columns as if finding in them motherly comfort, having gathered here perhaps because it was the only place they were allowed in, or because they yearned to be among the crowds of people, or because here there was water to drink and some hope of scraps of food being tossed their way. Already by the beginning of September someone had started selling burned sugar dissolved in a drum of water for fifty sen a cupful under the railway arches, and almost overnight a black market had sprung up offering steamed sweet potatoes, sweet potato dumplings, rice balls, bean jam rice cakes, fried rice, bean soup, bean jam buns, udon noodles, tempura and rice, curry and rice, then cake, rice, barley, sugar, tempura, beef, milk, canned fish, rice liquor, whisky, pears, bitter summer oranges, gum boots, bicycle inner tubes, matches, cigarettes, rubber-soled work shoes, nappies, army blankets, army boots, army uniforms, boots. A man stood holding out the aluminium lunchbox of barley rice his wife had packed for him just that morning – 'Yours for ten yen, yours for ten yen!' and another dangled his worn-out shoes in one hand – 'Twenty yen, how about it? Twenty yen!' Drawn purely by the smell of food, without any particular expectations, Seita had stumbled aimlessly in and had somehow managed to keep the wolf from the door for a couple of weeks by selling the underkimono, sash, collar and waist tie that were the only mementos he had of his mother from the flooded air-raid shelter, the colours faded and run, at a second-hand clothing stall consisting of a single straw mat spread out on the ground – then went his rayon middle school blazer, gaiters and shoes, and by the time he started wondering whether he could go so far as to sell his trousers, he was already a nightly fixture inside the station. Here a boy with his family apparently returning from evacuation to the countryside, fully decked out with his air raid hood neatly folded away over his canvas bag, his mess tin and kettle and steel helmet attached to his backpack, left him some mouldy ricebran dumplings, no doubt emergency food prepared for the train journey and now it was no longer needed, discarded to lighten the load. He gratefully accepted the crusts and roasted soybeans wrapped in paper placed quietly at a safe distance, as if making an offering to Buddha, by a kindly soldier returning from the front and an elderly woman with a grandson about his age who took pity on him. From time to time he was shooed away by the stationmaster, but the adjunct from the military police guarding the ticket gate protected him, shoving the man roughly away, and there was always enough water, so having found some comfort he settled in and put down roots until a couple of weeks later his legs gave out.

Assailed by severe diarrhoea, time after time he went to squat down over the station toilet, but then his legs gave way as he tried to get back up, and since the door handle was missing he had to push his body against the door in order to stand, and had to walk leaning on the wall with his hand for support. Decline set in like a deflating balloon, and before long he remained slouched against the column, no longer able to get up. Still the relentless attacks of diarrhoea continued and to his shame a yellow stain soon spread around his buttocks, and unable to run away he hastened to cover up the colour with what little sand and dust he could scoop from the floor with his hand. Nevertheless, he could only reach so far, and anyone who saw him probably thought he was just a war orphan crazed with hunger amusing himself with the shit seeping from his own body.

He no longer suffered from hunger, nor from thirst, and sat with his head slumped heavily on his chest, only his ears alive to the sounds around him. 'Ugh, he's filthy!' 'Is he dead?' 'What a disgrace, having the likes of him in the station when the American forces are about to arrive!' Then came the sudden quiet of night, the clip-clop of geta walking around the station, the rumble of trains passing overhead, footsteps abruptly setting off at a run, a child calling for his mother, a man muttering something next to him, the sound of the stationmaster throwing a bucket, 'What day is it today?' What day was it? How long had he been here? Suddenly he was aware of the concrete floor right before his eyes, not realizing that he had fallen with his body still in the L-shape it made when sitting upright, and his gaze fixed on the slight flutter of the dust on the floor with each weak breath, wondering only what day was it today . . . what day was it . . . Seita died.

It was late at night on 21 September 1945,

the day after the 'Protective Measures for War-Displaced Orphans and Other Persons' had been enacted, when the stationmaster gingerly searched Seita's lice-ridden clothes and found a small candy tin tucked into his bellyband; he tried to open it, but the lid was rusted on and didn't budge. 'What the heck is this?' 'What does it matter? Just chuck it!' 'And what about this kid too? Won't be long. It's all over once their eyes get that wide-open stare,' said another attendant, peering into the downturned face of an even younger war orphan sat beside Seita's dead body, which had been left there as it was for the city council to take away, not even covered in a straw mat. The candy tin rattled as the stationmaster shook it, then not knowing what to do with it he hurled it out of the station into the darkness of the burned-out ruins, already covered in thickly growing weeds. As it hit the ground the top flew off and white powder spilled out along with three small bone fragments, and twenty or thirty fireflies rose up from the grass in a flurry and flew around flashing on and off before eventually subsiding again.

The white bones belonged to Seita's little sister Setsuko, who had died on 22 August in the air-raid shelter tunnelled into the hillside at Manchitani in Nishinomiya. The cause of death was given as acute enteritis, but in reality at only four years old she had been so weakened by malnutrition that she had been unable to stand and had succumbed in her sleep, same as her brother.

On 5 June, Kobe had been attacked by a formation of 350 B29s, and the districts of Fukiai, Ikuta, Nada and Suma had been completely burned down to rubble, along with a large swathe of the eastern side of the city. As a third-year middle student, Seita had been mobilized to work in the Kobe Steelworks, but due to power-saving measures that day he was at home near the beach at Mikage when the standby alert for an air raid sounded, so as had long been drummed into him he had hastily placed the Seto ceramic brazier in a hole dug amongst the tomatoes, aubergines, cucumbers and edible greens growing in the back garden, then stored away whatever provisions he could find in the kitchen, rice, eggs, soybeans, dried bonito shavings, butter, dried herring, umeboshi, saccharine, dried eggs, and covered it all up with soil. He then hoisted Setsuko on his back as his mother was sick and too weak to carry her, removed the photo of his father – a lieutenant in the Imperial Navy stationed out of contact on a warship – in full dress uniform from its frame and tucked it into his shirt. He knew from the two previous air raids on 17 March and 11 May that it would be impossible to extinguish the incendiary bombs if you had a woman and a child to protect, and that the shelter dug under their house would not be of any use, so he first evacuated his mother to the concrete-reinforced shelter set up by the neighbourhood association at the rear of the fire station, then took his father's civilian clothes from the chest of drawers and was just stuffing them into his backpack when the bells on the air raid observation posts began ringing all at once sounding strangely cheerful, *kan-kan kin-kin*, and he dashed out of the front door only to be immediately enveloped in the sound of the bombs falling. After the first wave had passed, he had the illusion that a sudden stillness had fallen amidst the horror of that sound, but then the thunderous roar of B29s came relentlessly pressing down on him and he looked up. Until then, he had only seen them as barely discernible dots headed east leaving vapour trails, and during an air raid on Osaka just five days before weaving through the clouds over Osaka Bay like a shoal of fish, but now they were right overhead, huge, and so close he could even make out the thick line painted on the underbelly as they headed from the sea to the mountains then abruptly tilted their wings and disappeared westwards, and then once again the sound of bombs falling and he stood petrified as if the air had abruptly become too dense to move in, there was a clatter as something blue fell from the roof, an incendiary bomb five centimetres wide and sixty centimetres long went bouncing up and down the road like an inchworm spraying oil. He darted back inside in a panic, but already black smoke was slowly spreading through the house so he went back out where the street looked the same as ever, not a soul in sight, a fire broom and ladder leaned against the fence of the house opposite, so for the time being he decided to join his mother in the shelter and hoisted Setsuko up onto his back to set off when abruptly black smoke burst out of an upstairs window of the house on the corner, and as if on cue incendiary bombs that must have been smouldering in the attics all burst into flames and the garden trees crackled and popped, flames sped along the eaves, burning storm shutters came loose and fell off, everything went dark before his eyes and the air around him was burning, and he took off at a run as though propelled from behind. Thinking to escape as previously agreed to the banks of the Ishiya River, he headed eastwards alongside the elevated tracks of the

Hanshin Electric Railway, but the area was already jammed with people evacuating, some pulling hand carts and others carrying rolled-up bedding on their backs, the shrill voice of an old woman calling someone. Growing impatient, he instead headed towards the sea, sparks still falling all around and surrounded by the sound of falling bombs. A 5,000-litre sake barrel used for storing water smashed open, flooding the place with water, sick people were being carried out on stretchers, and though he passed one block without seeing a single person, the next was in uproar like at the time of the community clean-up, with people even carrying out tatami mats, so he took the old highway and then darted through the narrow streets of a deserted neighbourhood, nobody at all in sight, everyone already having fled, and finally the familiar black buildings of the sake breweries of Nada-Gogo where, in summer, the smell of the sea hung over everything and peeping through the narrow gaps between them, not even two metres, you would have glimpses of the sand glittering in the summer sun and the deep blue sea, surprisingly high. But none of that now, nowhere to shelter here on the beach, just the water where he'd been reflexively drawn thinking they could escape the flames, and other evacuees who had fled here with the same thought, now huddled under fishing boats and the pulleys for heaving up the nets here and there along the fifty-metre stretch of sand. Seita walked westwards to the Ishiya River, where he hid in one of the hollows scattered here and there in the upper level of the riverbank built after the great flood of 1938; they had no cover here but at least he felt safer settled in the hole and he sat down, his heart pounding and his throat parched. He hadn't had time to even look back at Setsuko while fleeing, but now he loosened the ties of the back sling, took her in his arms and set her down, and just with that effort his knees shook and he almost fell, yet still Setsuko did not cry, but sat quietly in her small splash-patterned air raid hood, white shirt and monpe trousers with the pattern matching her hood, red flannel tabi and only one of the black lacquer geta she took such good care of, her doll and their mother's large old coin purse clutched in her hands.

Brother and sister huddled close in terror amidst the smell of burning, the crackling of fires carried on the wind horrifyingly close and the sound of falling bombs moving far off to the west like a shower of rain, then Seita remembered the two-toned bento lunch in his air raid bag that their mother had made this morning from the remains of the plain white rice she had prepared the night before, saying there was no point in saving it, along with some whole grain rice with soybeans, already covered in a light sheen of condensation. Giving the white rice to Setsuko he looked up at the sky, and seeing it tinted orange he remembered their mother once telling him that on the morning of the Kanto Great Earthquake the clouds had turned yellow. 'Where's Mama?' 'She's in the shelter, the one behind the fire station. It can take a hit from a 250-kilogram bomb, so don't worry,' he said as if to convince himself, but he could see through the row of pine trees on the riverbank that the entire stretch of Hanshin Bay still flickered red and thought no, she must have escaped the flames, so added, 'She'll probably be at the twin pines on the Ishiya River by now, so let's go there after we've had a rest.' Then he asked, 'Are you okay, Setsuko? Did you get hurt at all?' 'I lost one of my geta.' 'I'll buy you another one, a better one.' 'I've got some money too,' she said, showing him the coin purse. 'Look!' He opened the strong metal clasp to find three or four one-sen and five-sen coins, along with a small white-spotted bean bag and a red, yellow and blue glass marble, the same one that a year ago Setsuko had swallowed and they had spread out some newspaper in the garden for her to poo on, and out it had come the following evening. 'Has our house burned down?' 'Probably.' 'What are we going to do?' 'Papa'll get revenge for us,' he said, quite beside the point, but who knew what would happen now? The sound of the bombing had finally receded and suddenly there was a squall like an evening rain shower, it lasted just five minutes, but seeing the black stains it left he thought, 'Oh, this must be what everyone always says falls after an air raid,' and at last his fear abated. He stood up and looked out to sea, and in just that short time its entire surface had become dirty and black from a vast amount of floating debris bobbing up and down, the mountains unchanged, perhaps a wildfire to the left of Mount Ichino, where purple smoke hung somewhat leisurely over it. 'Alrighty, up you get again,' he said, sitting Setsuko on the bank and turning his back to her so she could lean over onto him, and though he hadn't been aware of it while they were fleeing, she now felt like a dead weight as he crawled up the bank clutching onto clumps of grass.

From the top of the bank, Mikage First and Second Elementary schools and Mikage Town Hall looked so close it was as though they had upped and walked this way, the sake breweries and the military barracks, and also the fire station and the pine grove had all vanished, the embankment of the Hanshin Railway was right there before them, and three tram carriages, linked together, were stranded on the national highway. It looked as though the burned-out ruins continued up the slope to the foothills of Mount Rokko, which were hazy with smoke. Fifteen or sixteen places were still belching flames and smoke, and there was a whump as an unexploded incendiary device or time bomb went off and instantly a whooshing sound like a winter gale as a whirlwind sent a tin roof up into the sky. Feeling Setsuko cling ever more tightly to him, he said, 'See how nicely it's all been cleaned up! Look! That's the Town Hall where you came with me to eat rice and vegetable porridge,' but she didn't answer. He told her to wait a moment while he adjusted his gaiters, then set off walking along the top of the embankment again, on their right were three burned-out houses, all that was left of the Hanshin Ishiyagawa Station roof was the frame, and the shrine beyond it had been flattened with only the font of purifying water at the entrance remaining. Gradually they started to see more and more people, families slumped exhausted at the side of the road, only their mouths busily talking to each other, kettles hung from the end of sticks heating water over smouldering coals, roasting dried sweet potatoes. The twin pines were on the right further up the national highway headed towards the mountains, but when they finally reached them there was no sign of their mother, and everyone was peering down onto the dry riverbed so Seita looked and saw five drowned corpses on the sand, lying face down or spreadeagled on their backs, and felt the urge to confirm she wasn't among them.

After giving birth to Setsuko, his mother's heart had weakened and she would suffer spasms in the middle of the night, so she had Seita cool her chest with water, and when it hurt too much she would raise herself up to lean on the cushions he piled up for her, and he could see her left breast quivering with her heartbeat even under her nightwear. The only medicine available was Chinese herbs, a red powder to swallow morning and night, her wrists so thin he could wrap his hands twice around them. She couldn't run, so he had taken her to the shelter first despite knowing that it might end up being her final resting place if surrounded by the flames, and once the shortcut to the shelter had been cut off he'd made his escape at top speed without a second thought for her safety, and now he reproached himself – but even had he managed to get there what could he have done? 'Be sure to escape with Setsuko, I'll manage somehow on my own. If I can't get the two of you to safety, what will I tell your father? You do understand, don't you?' she'd told him jokingly.

Two naval trucks rushed westwards along the national highway, a man from the civil defence unit on a bicycle was shouting something into a megaphone, 'Got two direct hits, thought of covering them with a straw mat but they're leaking oil,' a boy about his age was saying to a friend, 'Everyone from Kaminishi,

Kaminaka and Ichirizuka, please assemble at Mikage National School,' hearing the name of his neighbourhood it immediately occurred to him that their mother might have taken refuge at the school, and was about to go down the embankment when there was another explosion, the flames were still raging in the rubble and they'd be blasted with heat on all but the widest roads. 'Let's stay here a bit longer,' he said to Setsuko, and as though she had been waiting for him to say something, she said, 'I need to pee,' so he set her down in the long grass and held her legs while her urine gushed out with surprising force, then he wiped her with his hand towel. 'You can take your hood off now,' and seeing her face was covered in soot, he dampened one end of the hand towel with water from his flask saying, 'This bit is clean,' as he cleaned her up. 'My eyes hurt!' They were red and bloodshot, maybe from the smoke. 'They'll wash them for you when we go to the school.' 'What happened to Mama?' 'She's at the school.' 'So let's go there!' 'We will, but it's still too hot to walk,' and Setsuko started crying saying she wanted to go to the school, sounding neither whiny nor in pain, but strangely grown up.

'Seita, have you seen your mother?' the daughter from the house opposite theirs, by now an old maid, called out to him in the school yard where he'd had an army medic clean Setsuko's eyes, but they still hurt so they'd joined the back of the queue again. 'Uh-uh.' 'You'd better go see her quick, she was injured,' and before he could ask, she said, 'I'll take care of Setsuko, it was scary, wasn't it, Setchan? Did you cry?' They hadn't been on particularly friendly terms before, and seeing how extraordinarily kindly she was treating them now he thought she must know his mother was in a bad way, so he hastily left the queue and headed for the sick room that he knew so well from having studied at the school for six years to find the sink full of something the colour of blood, scraps of bandages, the floor, the nurse's white gown, everything awash with blood, a man in national civil uniform lying face down utterly motionless, a woman whose monpe trousers had been cut away leaving one leg exposed and wrapped in bandages, and as he stood there in silence not knowing what to ask Mr Obayashi, the president of the neighbourhood association, said, 'Ah, Seita, there you are. I've been looking for you. You okay?' and putting his hand on his shoulder, 'This way,' guided him out into the corridor, then went back into the sick room and took a jade ring, cut off from a finger, out of some gauze in a kidney dish, 'This is your mother's, isn't it?' and he did indeed recognize it.

The seriously wounded were accommodated in the art room at the end of the ground floor, with those on the verge of death laid out in the teacher's room within, and this is where his mother lay, her upper body swathed in bandages, her hands resembling baseball bats, her face too wound round with bandages leaving only black holes around her eyes, nose and mouth, the tip of her nose like fried tempura batter, and he vaguely recognized her monpe now charred black with her camel-coloured long underwear showing through from beneath. 'She's asleep at last, but we must get her to a hospital. I've been asking around and heard the Nishinomiya Kaisei Hospital didn't burn.' She was not so much asleep as comatose, her breathing irregular. 'Um, Mama's got a bad heart, can you get some medicine for her?' 'Ah, okay, I'll see what I can do.' But even Seita knew it would be impossible. Next to his mother lay a man who had bubbles of blood erupting from his nose and mouth every time he breathed; a girl in a sailor blouse school uniform glanced around the room uncomfortably as she wiped it away with a hand towel, maybe unable to stand the sight, and beyond them a middle-aged woman whose lower body was exposed with just a small piece of gauze placed over her private parts, her left leg gone below the knee. 'Mama?' he called quietly but he barely had any sense of her, and for now he had

Setsuko to worry about, so he went back out into the schoolyard where he found her with the young woman in the sandpit with horizontal bars. 'Did you find her?' 'Uh huh.' 'You poor things. Just let me know if there is anything I can do. Did you get your rations of Kanpan biscuits?' He shook his head, and she set off saying she would go and get some for them, Setsuko all the while playing with an ice cream scoop she'd picked up out of the sand. 'Keep this ring in your purse. Make sure you don't lose it,' he said, putting it in the coin purse. 'Mama getting her chest pains again, but she'll be better soon.' 'Where is she?' 'In hospital at Nishinomiya. So today you and me'll stay here in the school, and tomorrow we'll go to our aunt in Nishinomiya, you remember her, don't you? In the house by the pond.' Setsuko quietly carried on playing at making shapes out of sand. 'My family's in a second-floor classroom. We're all there, so come join us,' the young woman said as she returned carrying two brown paper bags of biscuits, but Seita was worried that Setsuko would feel miserable being with a family that still had both parents, and in fact he himself felt he might start crying at any moment, so he replied that they would join them later. 'Here, eat some of these,' he said, offering the crackers to Setsuko. 'I want to go see Mama.' 'Maybe tomorrow, it's already late now,' he said, sitting down on the edge of the sand pit, then jumped up to the horizontal bar and said 'Look at me! I'm good at this!' as he hauled his body up onto it and started doing forward spins round and round; he had set a new record of forty-six forward spins on this very bar in the morning of 8 December, the day the war started.

The next day, he wanted to take their mother to hospital, but he couldn't very well carry her on his back so he hired a rickshaw near Rokko Michi Station, which had survived the fire. 'Hop on, I'll take you to the school,' the puller told him, and for the first time in his life he rode a rickshaw as they ran through the burned-out streets, but when they arrived she was already in a critical condition and it was impossible to move her, so the rickshaw puller refused the fare, waving it away with his hand as he left, and that evening she was so weakened from her burns that she drew her last breath. 'Please remove her bandages and let me see her face,' Seita asked, and the doctor, now in his military medic uniform having removed his white coat, told him 'Better not see, it's for the best.' His heavily bandaged mother, utterly still, flies swarming around her bandages seeped with blood, the man who'd been blowing blood bubbles, the woman who'd lost a leg – all had died, and a policeman briefly asked the bereaved families a few questions and wrote something down, then said to no one in particular, 'All we can do is dig a hole in the grounds of the Rokko Crematorium and burn them there, and we'll have to take them by truck tonight, given this warm weather,' then saluted and left. There were no flowers or incense, or the makura-dango rice dumplings usually placed as an offering, or sutra chanting, not even anyone to cry for them, one woman from the bereaved families, her eyes tightly shut, was having her hair combed by an old woman, another put a baby to her bare breast to drink, and a boy with an already crumpled extra of a tabloid paper in one hand exclaimed admiringly, 'A whopping sixty per cent of those 350 planes in the raid were shot down!' and though it had nothing to do with his mother's death Seita too calculated in his head that sixty per cent of 350 planes meant 210 planes.

For the time being he left Setsuko with their distant relative in Nishinomiya, a widow who had exchanged a promise with their mother that if either house were burned down they would help each other, who lived with her son, who was a student at the Merchant Marine School, and her daughter, and also a lodger who worked at the customs house in Kobe. His mother's body was to be cremated from noon on 7 June at the foot of Mount Ichinosan, so they removed the bandages from her wrists and attached a name tag with wire, he finally saw his mother's skin blackened and discoloured, hardly like anything human, and as they lifted her onto the stretcher, maggots tumbled out of her and then he realized there were hundreds and thousands of maggots crawling around the art room floor, all being casually squashed underfoot as the bodies were carried out, those burned black like logs were wrapped and piled onto a truck, those who had died from suffocation or injuries were left uncovered and laid out in a row on a bus from which the seats had been removed.

In an open space below Mount Ichinosan, a hole with a diameter of about ten metres had been filled with ridge poles, beams, shoji and fusuma retrieved from evacuated buildings, and the bodies placed on top, then some civilian guards dashed buckets of fuel oil over it all like in fire drills, lit a rag and threw it in, and immediately black smoke rose up as the blaze took hold, and whenever a burning body rolled off it was dragged back into the fire with a firefighter's pike pole, and beside it all a table covered in a white cloth, with several hundred simple wooden boxes ready to hold the bones.

The families had been sent away as they would just be in the way, not even a mendicant monk had been in attendance, but that night after it was over, he went to collect a wooden box, the name written in cinders – had that name tag been of any use? – that contained a finger bone that was starkly white in contrast to the black smoke of the cremation.

It was late at night by the time he finally reached the house in Nishinomiya. 'Is Mama still in pain?' 'Yes, she was injured in the air raid.' 'Won't she be wearing her ring any more? Did she give it to me?' He suddenly had a vision of the ring being worn on the white finger bone in the wooden box he'd hidden in the shutter pocket above the ornamental shelves and he hastily brushed it aside. 'It's precious, so we'd better put it away,' he said to Setsuko as she sat on a floor cushion playing with the marble and the ring. Unknown to Seita, his mother had already taken the precaution of sending along kimono, bedding and mosquito nets to this house. 'You have it good in the navy, being able to take things by truck,' the widow had said with no trace of irony as she showed him the luggage covered in arabesque-patterned cloth in a corner of the corridor, and he opened a wicker box to find everything from underwear for himself and Setsuko to some of his mother's regular clothes, and in a cardboard dress box were some formal long-sleeved kimonos and the smell of mothballs that filled him with nostalgia.

They were allotted a small, three tatami mat room beside the entrance hall, and given a certificate of war victims that enabled them to get special rations of rice and tinned salmon, beef, and beans. Once the burned-out ruins had cooled down he had managed to locate the surprisingly tiny plot he thought was where they had lived, and had dug the spot he thought most likely and found the food he'd stored away with the ceramic brazier. He borrowed a handcart and crossed four rivers, the Ishiya, Sumiyoshi,

Ashiya and Shukugawa, taking a whole day to carry them and pile them up in the entrance hall, but again the widow had grumbled, 'Only military families enjoy such luxury, eh?' while delightedly showing the goods off, even sharing some of the umeboshi with the neighbours, and since the water supply was still cut off she must have been happy to have a boy around to help draw water from the well 300 metres away, so her daughter currently in year four of her girls' school and mobilized to Nakajima Aircraft even took some days off work to care for Setsuko.

At the well, the wife of a local soldier away at the front became the subject of gossip in the neighbourhood when she was seen boldly holding hands with a student of Doshisha University who was half naked and wearing his school cap, while Seita and Setsuko aroused local sympathy as the children of a navy lieutenant who had tragically lost their mother in the air raid since the widow was making it known at every opportunity that she was doing them a favour.

As night fell, the loud booming cries of the bullfrogs came from the reservoir close by, and fireflies perched on the tips of the grasses growing thickly either side of the fast-flowing stream flickered on and off, so Seita reached out and took one in his hand where it glowed within his fingers. 'Here, try holding it,' he said, putting it on Setsuko's palm, but she squeezed it so hard she crushed it and immediately an acrid smell spread over her hands. In the humid darkness of the June night, though Nishinomiya was still part of the city, they were by the mountain and the air raids felt like something far away that affected other people.

They had once sent a letter to their father care of the Kure Naval District, although no answer came, and on their way home he'd persuaded his mother to drop by their bank, so he now recalled the Kobe Bank Rokko branch and the Sumitomo Bank Motomachi branch and went to check the balances, and when he told the widow that there was just 7,000 yen in them, she boasted, 'When my husband died, his retirement allowance was 70,000 yen,' and went on to brag about her son, 'Yukihiko was only in year three of middle school, but everyone was impressed by the way he greeted the company president, he's so dependable that boy.' It sounded like a snide remark at Seita, who found it hard to fall asleep at night and would sometimes cry out in fear and wake up again, and would then get up late. And in just ten days the pickled plums in the wide-mouthed jar, and the dried eggs and butter had all gone, the special rations for disaster victims had also gone, and even the 330-gram rice ration was now half soy bean, wheat or corn, but given the hearty appetite of growing children the widow suspected that they were eating into her family's share too, and soon started digging the ladle deep into the rice gruel they had for all three meals to scoop up the rice at the bottom for her daughter, putting just watery soup and greens in the bowls for Seita and Setsuko, now and then saying, 'My girl here is working for the nation and needs to eat to keep her strength up, after all,' as though to allay her conscience. He could always hear her in the kitchen using the ladle to scrape the charred rice off the bottom of the pan, those crusty bits that were full of flavour, smelled so good, and were nice and chewy, and he didn't so much feel angry at the greedy widow as sensed his saliva welling up. The lodger who worked in the customs house knew all about the black market and would give the widow beef, malt syrup and canned salmon to curry her favour, his eyes on her daughter.

'Shall we go to the seaside?' he asked Setsuko one day in the rainy season when the weather was clear, worried about her terrible heat rash and thinking that rinsing it with seawater was bound to make it better. He didn't know what was going through her child's mind but she no longer talked about their mother and now simply clung to him. 'Yes, let's go!' Until last summer they had rented a room in Suma for the summer; he would leave Setsuko on the beach and swim out to see the glass weights on the fishing nets floating out at sea, and there was a teahouse on the beach where they were served amazake that smelled of ginger as they blew on it to cool it down, and later they would eat the powdered roast barley and sugar their mother made, Setsuko stuffing her mouth with it and ending up choking with powder all over her face, and he was about to ask her if she remembered that but then thought better of carelessly reminding her.

They headed for the beach along a stream, past horse-drawn carts transporting the luggage of evacuees stopped here and there on the straight asphalt road, a plump boy wearing glasses and a cap from Kobe Prefectural Middle School had his arms full of difficult-looking books, and the horse flicked its tail listlessly as he put them on the back of a cart; turning right they came to the banks of the Shukugawa River, on the way there had been a coffee shop called Pavoni which sold agar jelly flavoured with saccharine, so they'd stop in for some. It reminded him of Jucheim's in Sannomiya that had continued selling cake until the end, and six months ago when they announced they were closing the shop they'd made some decorated fancy cakes, and their mother had bought one. The owner of that place had been Jewish, and Seita recalled that a lot of Jewish refugees had come to Akayashiki near Shinohara where he used to go to learn arithmetic around 1940, and though they were all young they had beards, and at four o'clock in the afternoon they would queue up outside the bathhouse, wearing heavy overcoats despite the summer heat, and one was wearing two left shoes and limped, what had happened to them, he wondered, must be prisoners of war sent to the factory. The prisoners worked harder than anyone, it was said, first the prisoners, second the students, third the drafted workers, fourth the factory employees, while the trade professionals wasted their time making cigarette cases out of duralumin or rulers out of synthetic resins, was that going to help win the war? The embankment of the Shukugawa River had been entirely turned over to vegetable gardens, with kabocha and cucumber flowers blooming, nobody in sight all the way to the main road, and stashed away in a wooded area along the road for use in the final battle for the mainland was an intermediate training plane sitting quietly beneath a sorry excuse for camouflage netting. On the beach they could see the figures of an old woman and a child scooping up seawater into a large bottle. 'Setsuko, take your clothes off,' Seita told her, 'This might feel a bit cold,' as he soaked his hand towel in the water again and again, washing the dense red rash covering her shoulders and thighs already looking plump and girlish; the neighbour two doors down from the widow's house in Manchitani let them use the bath, but they were always the last and in the dark of the blackouts they couldn't wash themselves properly, but seeing her bare skin now she was white like their father. 'Oh, what happened to him? Is he asleep?' she asked, and he looked down at the low sea wall and saw a dead body covered in a rush mat, the two legs sticking out appeared so much bigger than the body, 'Don't look at that. When it gets a bit

warmer we'll be able to swim. I'll teach you.'
'If we go swimming we'll get hungry.' Seita had been so unbearably hungry lately that he would squeeze a pimple and instinctively put the white fat in his mouth without thinking, he had money but didn't know how to buy things on the black market. 'Maybe I should try fishing?' Surely he'd be able to catch wrasse and flatheads or at least pick some seaweed, but all he found was rotten sargassum undulating forlornly in the waves.

A siren sounded so they started to head back and were just passing the Kaisei Hospital when suddenly a young woman's voice rang out, 'Oh, Mother!' and he looked around to see a nurse embracing a middle-aged woman carrying a cloth bag, a mother come from the countryside, and Seita gazed absently at the sight of them, half envious, and half thinking how pretty the nurse's expression was, but then he heard 'Take refuge!' and abruptly looked up to see B29s flying low over the sea off Osaka Bay dropping sea mines. Maybe their target had already burned, there hadn't been any large-scale air raids lately.

'I'm sorry to say this, Seita, but you don't have any need for your mother's kimonos now, so why not exchange them for some rice? I've also been exchanging things little by little, to supplement our rations,' the widow said, adding that his deceased mother would be pleased. She must have already gone through everything while he'd been out, and before he could say anything she went ahead opening the clothes boxes with a practised hand, took out two or three kimonos, and threw them down on the tatami, 'You should be able to get one toh of rice for this. You need nutrition too, Seita, so you can grow strong and become a soldier.'

They were kimonos from when his mother was young, and he remembered how once when she had attended a class on parents' day, Seita had turned to look at her and confirmed that she was the most beautiful woman there and had been filled with pride, and when they went to Kure to see his father, his mother had looked surprisingly youthful as they rode the train together, so happy that he couldn't help touching it, but now just hearing the words 'one toh of rice' he felt such an intense joy well up that his body started trembling; the infrequent rations of rice for both him and Setsuko did not fill even half a shallow bamboo dish, but they had to make it last for five days.

The area around Manchitani was populated with farmhouses, and when the widow finally came home with a bag of rice, she filled Seita's wide-necked umeboshi jar, then poured the rest into the wooden rice bin for her own family's use. They ate their fill for two or three days before going back to simple rice gruel, and when he grumbled about it being unfair she said, 'Seita, you're a big boy now, you should think of ways we can help each other. If you don't contribute any rice but still demand to be fed, it just isn't right. It won't do.' Whether it would do or not, she was happily using the rice exchanged for his mother's kimono to make her daughter's lunch box and rice balls for the lodger, while only giving the two of them fried rice mixed with defatted soybeans, which Setsuko didn't want to eat having been reminded of the taste of rice. 'How can you say that? That's our rice!' 'What? Are you suggesting I'm cheating you? What a thing to say! Having taken in two orphans only to be spoken to like that, it's really too much. Look, how about we eat separately, that way you won't have anything to complain about. And by the way, Seita, you've got relatives in Tokyo too, haven't you? What's his name, that one on your mother's side, how about sending him a letter? You never know when Nishinomiya will get bombed too.' She hadn't actually told him to leave right away, but on the other hand, from her point of view they had taken the liberty of moving in on her and then staying on and on, and after all it was the family home of their father's cousin's wife, and they had closer relatives in Kobe, but since everything had burned down he hadn't managed to contact them. At a household goods store he bought a ladle made from a shell with a handle attached to it, an earthenware cooking pot, a soy sauce dispenser, and since they were selling boxwood combs for ten yen he bought one for Setsuko. Morning and night he borrowed the charcoal brazier and cooked rice, and to go with it boiled purslane and kabocha stems with pond snails simmered in soy sauce and dried squid reconstituted in hot water. 'It's okay, no need to be so formal,' he told Setsuko, seeing her kneeling properly as she had always been taught as they settled down to their meagre fare placed directly on the tatami without even a tray, and when Seita stretched out on the floor after eating she warned him, 'You'll turn into a lazy cow if you do that!' Cooking separately was less stressful, but he couldn't keep on top of everything and somehow she'd managed to pick up lice that fell along with their eggs out of her hair when he ran the boxwood comb through it, and when he washed their clothes and thoughtlessly hung them outside to dry, the widow grumbled, 'The enemy planes'll see them there.' He was desperately doing his best but they somehow became covered in grime and on top of that could no longer use the neighbour's bath, so could only go to the public bath once every three days as long as they provided fuel to heat the water and this too ended up being tedious. By day he would just lie down reading a woman's magazine his mother used to read, which he'd bought at a secondhand bookstore by Shukugawa Station, and if a warning sounded and the radio announced that it was a large formation, he didn't want to go into the rudimentary local shelter so fled with Setsuko on his back to a tunnel shelter dug deep into the hillside the other side of the pond, earning the disapproval not just of the widow but of other neighbours already tired of war orphans. At Seita's age he should be a core member of the neighbourhood fire-fighting activities, but having experienced firsthand the sound of the bombs falling and the speed at which the fire spread, he would have baulked at the sight of even one or two planes, and had no intention of confronting a large formation.

On 6 July, in the rain lingering on from the rainy season, the B29s attacked Akashi, and Seita and Setsuko were in the tunnel shelter gazing vacantly at the ripples on the pond caused by a passing shower, Setsuko clutching the doll that was always with her. 'I want to go home, I don't like being at Auntie's place,' she sobbed, although she had hardly complained before. 'Our house burned down, it's not there any more.' Still, they probably wouldn't be able to spend much longer at the widow's house, at night Setsuko would cry out in fear during some nightmare, and as if she'd been waiting the widow would come in and say, 'My daughter and the lodger are working for the country, aren't they? Can't you at least stop her from crying like that? They won't be able to get any sleep,' before slamming the fusuma shut as she left, but her threats merely made Setsuko cry even more so he would take her outside, where the fireflies were out as always. It briefly occurred to him how much easier things would be if Setsuko weren't here, but as she fell asleep the moment he put her on his back she suddenly felt lighter to him, the mosquitos were voraciously feeding on her face and arms, and the bites would fester and pus oozed out whenever she scratched them. Some time before that when the widow was out, Seita had opened up her daughter's old reed organ and started playing 'he-to-i-ro-ha-ro-i-ro-to-ro-i, he-to-i-ro-i-he-ni': the do-re-mi musical notation had been abolished under the new school system introduced in 1941, and he clumsily played the first song he'd learned in the new notation, the Carp Streamers song, and was singing along with Setsuko when suddenly the widow came home. 'Stop that right now! What do you think you're doing? We're at war! I'm the one who'll get into trouble about this. Where's your common sense?' she shouted, 'What a terrible plague has visited us! You're not even of any use in the air raids. If you value your life that much you might as well go live in that tunnel!'

'What do you think? Shall we make this our

home? Nobody'll come bothering us here, and with just the two of us we can do as we please.' The tunnel shelter had been dug into the slope in a right-angled U-shape and was supported by thick stays, they could buy some straw from a farmer and spread it out to sleep on, hang the mosquito net up, and they'd be okay like that – it was a bit of excitement, like going on an adventure as boys of his age did, so when the air raid warning was lifted he went to the house and packed up their things without a word. 'Sorry to have stayed so long, we're going to live somewhere else,' 'What do you mean, somewhere else? Where are you going?' 'I'm not sure yet,' 'Really? Well, take care of yourselves. Goodbye Setchan,' she said putting on a contrived smile and, turning on her heel, went back inside.

Somehow he managed to carry the wicker case, futon, mosquito net, kitchen things, as well as the clothes box and the wooden box with their mother's remains to the shelter, but seeing it now in a new light it was just a cave, and his spirits sank at the thought of living there, but then a farmer he asked at random shared some straw with them and sold them some tree onions and a daikon radish, and best of all Setsuko started rushing around excitedly, 'This will be the kitchen. Here's the front entrance.' Abruptly she stopped, disconcerted. 'What about the toilet?' 'Does it matter? You can do it wherever you want. I'll come with you.' Seeing her sitting upright on the straw he recalled his father saying 'This girl is going to be quite the refined beauty,' and when Seita didn't understand the word 'refined' he'd explained, 'Hmm, right, it means something like classy,' and it was true and she was all the more pitiful for it.

They were already used to the dark of the blackouts, but the pitch-black darkness of the night in the shelter was like another layer of black painted over everything; as he hung the mosquito net from the struts and they went inside, all they had to go on was the whine of the mosquitos clustering outside the net, and instinctively the two of them drew closer together. Seita hugged her bare feet to his belly, and abruptly felt a tingle of arousal and pulled her closer. 'That hurts,' she said, scared.

Unable to sleep, he suggested going for a walk so they went outside and both had a pee, above them passed the red and green flashing beacon lights of Japanese planes headed west, 'Those are kamikaze planes.' 'Uh huh,' Setsuko said, not knowing what he meant, 'They look like fireflies,' 'So they do.' While he wasn't consciously imitating the Chinese scholar Che Yin, who had famously studied by the light of fireflies, it occurred to him that he could catch some fireflies and put them inside the mosquito nets for a bit of light. He grabbed as many as he could and released them inside the net, and five or six lights meandered around before settling on the net flickering, and taking heart he continued until he had a hundred or so. It wasn't bright enough to see each other's faces, but they felt more at ease, and as he followed the gently moving lights he was drawn into a dream, the lines of light from the fireflies soon merging with the parade of ships in the naval review of October 1935, the large illuminated form of a ship on the flank of Mount Rokko from where he had gazed over Osaka Bay, the combined fleet and an aircraft carrier looking like sticks floating in the water, white drapes hung from the bows of battleships, and Seita desperately searched among the warships for any sight of the cruiser *Maya* that his father was currently aboard, but he couldn't see anything resembling the distinctive cliff-like bridge of the *Maya*, but he heard snatches of the 'Warship March' played by a brass band, maybe from the College of Commerce. *Defending and attacking, our reliable floating iron fortresses*, Papa's photograph was now heavily stained with sweat, where was he doing battle now? Enemy planes attacking *ba-ba-ba-ba-ba*, the light of the fireflies were like tracer bullets, oh yes, the tracer bullets from anti-aircraft guns the night of the air raid on 17 March had floated up into the sky like fireflies, but had they hit anything?

By morning, half the fireflies had died, and Setsuko buried their carcasses by the entrance to the shelter. 'What are you doing?' 'Making a grave for the fireflies,' she replied without looking up, and then, Mama's in a grave too, isn't she? and when he couldn't reply she said, 'I heard it from Auntie, Mama's dead and buried too,' and for the first time Seita felt tears well up. 'Let's go to her grave sometime, we've been to the Kasugano graveyard near Nunobiki, Setsuko, do you remember? That's where Mama is,' under a camphor tree, in a small grave, we should put this bone in there too, so that she can rest in peace.

Having been seen exchanging his mother's kimono for some rice at a farmhouse and drawing water, it soon became known the two of them were living in the shelter, but nobody came, and Seita gathered dry twigs to cook rice, and when they lacked salt he used seawater. He was shot at along the way by American P51 planes but otherwise the days were tranquil, and watched over by fireflies at night they grew accustomed to the passing of days in the shelter, but then Seita developed a rash between his fingers, and Setsuko too was growing steadily weaker. They would wait until nightfall to get into the reservoir to collect pond snails and as he washed Setsuko's body he could see her shoulder blades and ribs standing out more and more by the day. 'You have to eat more,' he told her, and he stared over to where the booming calls of the bullfrogs were coming from and wondered whether he could maybe catch some, but he didn't know how, and it was all very well saying she needed to eat more, but he had already come to the end of his mother's kimonos, and the prices on black market – one egg for three yen, a sho of oil for a hundred yen, a hundred monme of beef for twenty yen, a sho of rice for twenty-five yen – were way beyond reach unless you had connections. Since they were close to town the farmers were savvy and would not sell them rice for money, so before long they had gone back to soy bean gruel, and by the end of July Setsuko had caught scabies, and if he thought he'd managed to eliminate all the fleas and lice, the next morning the seams of their clothes were teeming with them again. Enraged at the thought that the red blood in those grey lice was Setsuko's, he amused himself by ripping off their tiny legs one by one before killing them but it wasn't any help, and he even wondered whether fireflies were edible. Eventually she grew listless and would see him off to the beach saying, 'I'll wait for you here,' and lie hugging her doll, and whenever Seita went out he would always steal from local vegetable gardens and come back with a cucumber the size of his little finger or a still-green tomato, which he would give to Setsuko to eat, and once he came across a boy of five or six biting into an apple that looked like a piece of treasure and so he snatched it and raced home, 'Setsuko, here, an apple for you!' and she bit into it, her eyes gleaming, but immediately said, no, it isn't an apple and when Seita took a bite he realized it was a raw peeled sweet potato and maybe from having unwittingly had her hopes raised her eyes filled with tears. 'Potato's good too, here, eat it – if you don't, I will,' he said sharply, but his voice too sounded nasal.

What happened to the rations? He had been given matches and rock salt along with rice, but the rations he read about in the newspapers from time to time were unavailable to him as he was not enrolled in the neighbourhood association, so when his nightly forages pilfering from the vegetable gardens weren't enough, he started venturing into the farmers' potato crops and pulling up sugarcane and giving the juice to Setsuko to drink.

On the night of 31 July, he was raiding a field when there was an air raid siren but he carried on digging up potatoes anyway, and was caught in the act by a farmer come to take refuge in a nearby open shelter and given a thrashing. When the warning was lifted the farmer marched him back to the tunnel shelter, where the light from his torch fell on the potato leaves he had left intending to use them in a stew, irrefutable proof. 'I'm sorry, please forgive me,' he apologized to the farmer, kneeling before him as Setsuko watched in terror. 'My little sister is sick, if I'm not here she will have no one to care for her,' but the farmer showed him no mercy. 'What the hell are you saying? Stealing from vegetable gardens during wartime is a serious crime,' then took him down with a foot sweep and grabbed him by the scruff of his neck, 'Step to it, we'll have you locked up.' The police officer on duty took it in his stride, saying only, 'Tonight it seems the air raid is in Fukui,' to placate the furious farmer, then gave Seita a lecture before letting him go, and he went outside to see Setsuko had somehow managed to follow them there. Together they went back to the shelter where Seita kept crying as Setsuko rubbed his back. 'Where does it hurt? It doesn't look good, we should call the doctor and have him give you an injection,' she said, sounding just like their mother.

As August came and planes from offshore

aircraft carriers made daily attacks, Seita waited for the air raid warnings to sound before going out to steal, waiting for the moment in which the residents ducked their heads as they fled to the shelters out of fear of the planes glittering in the distance in the summer sky and then were suddenly overhead and strafing fire down on them, to sneak in through open gates into kitchens pilfering whatever he could find. On the night of 5 August central Nishinomiya burned, and even the residents of Manchitani who were known for being placid were shaken, but this moment amid the terrible roar of the bombardment along with what sounded like explosions was the peak time for Seita, and he slipped into a part of the neighbourhood where there was no sign of even a single person left, much like he'd seen back on 5 June, and took kimonos that he could exchange for rice, a backpack left behind, carrying with him whatever he could and hiding what he couldn't carry under the stone covers of roadside gutters, all the while brushing off sparks then crouching down to avoid being seen by a surge of people fleeing, and as he looked up at the night sky at the sight of the B29s obscured by the smoke above the flames headed for the mountains and then turning towards the sea, there was nothing more to fear and he even felt like jeering and waving his arms at them.

In all the confusion he had managed to select a brightly coloured kimono that might be bartered for a good amount of food, and the next day with nothing to wrap it in he stuffed the eye-catching long-sleeved garment into his shirt and trousers and, with it slipping out as he walked, he hugged his belly bulging like a frog's, and went around farmhouses, but people in the countryside were already anticipating a poor rice harvest and were beginning to be reluctant to sell any, and knowing he would come under suspicion in the local area he had gone searching as far as northern Nishinomiya and Nigawa where even the rice fields had bomb craters in them, only to get some tomatoes, edamame and green beans.

Setsuko's diarrhoea wouldn't stop, the right side of her body was almost translucent white, the left festering with scabies, washing it with seawater made it sting and she cried. A doctor by Shukugawa Station merely said, 'She needs better nutrition,' and cursorily held a stethoscope to her chest and gave her no medicine, but instead explained that good sources of nutrition would be white fish, egg yolks, butter and maybe a Dorikono energy drink. Seita recalled coming home from school and finding in the post box a package of chocolate made in Shanghai sent by his father, and if he had an upset tummy he would drink the juice of an apple grated and strained through cloth. It felt like such a long time ago, but they'd been able to get hold of anything up until the year before last, no, even two months ago, their mother had stewed peaches in sugar and opened a can of crabmeat, he'd refused to eat red bean jelly saying it was too sweet, and he'd thrown away the Nanking bento, just plain rice with a single red umeboshi, on the Day of Public Duty for the Development of Asia, saying it smelled bad, and the awful shojin ryori vegetarian food at Obakusan Manpukuji Temple in Kyoto, how unpalatable it was the first time he'd eaten suiton dumplings in soup – all like a dream now.

Setsuko always carried her doll around with her wherever she went, its head wobbling as she walked, but now she no longer even had the strength to lift it – indeed the doll's limbs black with dirt were now plumper than hers. Seita sat down with her on the bank of the Shukugawa beside a man shaving ice loaded on a small trailer with a saw *shaa-shaa*; he picked up remnants of the shavings and moistened Setsuko's lips with them. 'I'm hungry.' 'Mmm.' 'What would you like to eat?' 'Tempura, and sashimi, and jelly noodles.' He'd never liked tempura, and he'd secretly thrown his portions to a dog they'd once had called Belle. 'What else?' Even just talking about what they wanted to eat and remembering the flavours was better than nothing; that time they'd gone to see a play in Dotonbori and on the way home had eaten seafood sukiyaki at Maruman, when they'd been given one egg each but his mother had given him hers; and that time he'd gone with his father to Chinatown for Chinese food on the black market, and when served candied sweet potatoes, he'd pulled the thin strands of sugar on top asking if it was rotten and everyone had laughed; and that time he'd pinched one of the 'black' candies they put in soldiers' comfort bags, and often used to pinch Setsuko's powdered milk, and cinnamon drops from the sweet shop; that time on a school trip when he'd shared his apple with one poor boy who only had Glico and ramune candies – but what was he thinking, he really had to get some nutrition into Setsuko, and feeling unbearably frustrated he picked her up again and went back to the shelter.

Watching Setsuko as she dozed, still hugging her doll, Seita thought of cutting off his finger so she could drink his blood, one finger wouldn't matter, she could eat the flesh off it. 'Setsuko, isn't your hair bothering you?'

Her hair alone was full of vitality, growing long and thick, he sat her up and braided it for her, and could feel the lice as he ran his fingers through it. 'Thank you, Seita,' she said, the hollows of her eye sockets even more pronounced with her hair tied back. She picked up two stones lying nearby, as though something had just occurred to her. 'Here you are, Seita.' 'What's that?' 'Dinner. Would you like some tea with it?' Now she was suddenly animated. 'And let me give you some stewed okara too,' she said, arranging clumps of earth and stones as if playing house. 'Here you are, please make yourself at home, won't you have something to eat?'

On the afternoon of 22 August, when he came back to the shelter after swimming in the reservoir, Setsuko was dead. She had wasted away to just skin and bones, had not spoken at all for two or three days, and though giant ants crawled over her face she didn't brush them away, only at night her eyes moved as though following the light of a firefly, murmuring quietly, 'Up it goes, down it goes, oh, now it stopped.' The previous week, when it had been announced that Japan had lost the war, Seita couldn't help shouting out, 'What happened to the Combined Fleet?' and an old man next to him had said full of confidence, 'That sank a long time ago, there's not a single ship left,' so that that must mean his father's cruiser had sunk too, he thought, gazing at the crumpled photo of his father that he carried next to his skin at all times. 'Papa's dead too, Papa's dead too.' He felt the loss of his father more keenly than that of his mother, and realizing only the two of them were left, he finally lost the will to keep himself and Setsuko alive, nothing mattered any more. But for Setsuko's sake he'd walked around the neighbouring districts and villages putting several of the ten-yen notes he took out of their savings into his pocket, now and then buying chicken meat for 150 yen, the price of rice had risen sharply and one sho cost forty yen, he'd tried to feed her some but she could no longer eat.

As night fell there was a storm, and Seita cowered in the darkness of the shelter with Setsuko's corpse on his lap, dozing off only to immediately wake up again; he stroked her hair and pressed his cheek against her already cold forehead, but the tears did not come. The wind howled, the leaves on the trees whipped back and forth, and as the storm raged he suddenly thought he could hear Setsuko crying, and was further assailed by an hallucination of the rousing strains of the 'Warship March'.

The next day, the typhoon had passed leaving in its wake a cloudless sky that had abruptly taken on hues of autumn, and Seita was bathed in sunshine as he carried Setsuko up the mountain. When he'd asked at the city office he was told the crematoriums were all full, they hadn't even dealt with all the cases from a week earlier, so he was given a special ration of a straw-wrapped bale of charcoal and told, 'Since she's a child, you can go to a corner in a temple grounds somewhere, they'll let you burn her there. Be sure to take her clothes off first, and if you add soybean husks the fire will catch well,' the man in the rations office told him, as though used to it.

On a hill overlooking Manchitani, he dug a hole, put Setsuko into the wicker basket and stuffed all her belongings, her doll, coin purse, underwear around her, then he did as he had been told and scattered soy bean husks into the hole, arranged some dried twigs over them and emptied the charcoal on top, then placed the wicker basket on top, lit a sulphur match, and threw it on top of it all. The soy bean husks crackled and popped as the fire caught, smoke swayed and then surged in a line up into the sky; he abruptly felt the urge to defecate and crouched down, watching the flames, struck with chronic diarrhoea.

As it grew dark, with each gust of wind the charcoal gave a low hum and flickered red, there were stars in the night sky, and looking down into the valley below where the blackouts had been lifted two days earlier, here and there he could see lights in the houses for the first time in a long time. Four years before he had walked around this area with his mother when she was looking into the background of a prospective marriage candidate for his father's cousin, and remembered gazing from a distance at that widow's house and nothing had changed in the slightest.

Later that night the fire burned out, but he couldn't see the bones to pick them up in the dark so he lay down right there beside the hole, a great number of fireflies swarming around him, but he no longer caught them in his hand; this way Setsuko wouldn't be lonely, the fireflies would be with her, flying up and down, darting sideways – they will be gone soon, but for now you can go to heaven with the fireflies. He awoke in the first light, collected the bones, broken up like small fragments of soapstone, and went down the mountain to the open-air air-raid shelter behind the widow's house where he found a sodden bundle, his mother's kimono undergarment and cord, probably discarded there by the widow after Seita had left without them, so he picked it up and put it on his back, and with that he left, never to return to the tunnel shelter by the pond.

In the afternoon of the 22 September 1945, having died an ignominious death in Sannomiya Station, Seita was cremated in a temple above Nunobiki together with the corpses of another twenty or thirty war orphans, and their bones were stored in the crypt as abandoned souls.

## Translator's Note

'Grave of the Fireflies' was first published in 1967 in the magazine *All Yomimono*, and together with 'American Hijiki' won Akiyuki Nosaka the prestigious Naoki Prize in 1967. The two stories along with four more were published in a collection in 1968. 'Grave of the Fireflies' is probably the closest Nosaka came to writing about his own experience of the Kobe firebombing of June 1945.

While many elements of the story are autobiographical, there are significant differences, the most important being that his protagonist, Seita, was an idealized character who acted far more nobly and cared much better for his little sister than Nosaka himself had been capable of. The lives of the two children in the story, aged fourteen and four, are portrayed as being as fleeting as the fireflies, and the story is an unsentimental and unflinching account with moments of both tenderness and heartlessness. Nosaka always regretted not caring better for his own sister, who was just sixteen months old when she died. He blamed himself, as he didn't share food with her, and he wrote the story to atone for her death and give repose to her soul. Of course, unlike Seita, he survived and went on to become a prolific author, singer, TV personality – and even politician – before his death in 2015.

The story was written at a time when the effects of the war were still very much in evidence, but people were moving on and trying to forget, working hard to pull the country out of poverty while beginning to see the economy heating up. It is written in an almost stream-of-consciousness style, rather like someone reluctantly dredging up their memories, with random thoughts interrupting the narrative, long sentences sometimes running to over a page, little punctuation, and peppered with Kobe dialect. The style, deliberately not easy to read even for

Japanese readers, is an important element of the story. However, given that James R. Abrams has already tried to capture the style and dialect in his translation published in the *Japan Quarterly* in 1978, which is still available to read online for anyone interested, I felt there was little point in taking a similar approach with my retranslation. Furthermore, readers of this new translation are in a time and space that is far removed from when the story was written, and many will have already seen the Ghibli animated film directed by Isao Takahata, which was released in 1988 and is currently streaming on Netflix. Instead of letting the sentences run on and on, therefore, I have sometimes broken them up to make it easier to follow the trains of thought, while attempting to maintain the breathlessness and confusion of the original. And rather than attempt to reflect the dialect, I have simply tried to capture the voices of the children and the various adults around them.

Interestingly, the penultimate paragraph of the original story was left out of the final published version, perhaps because one of the Naoki Prize judges had considered it somewhat old-fashioned.

> その夜、布引の谷あいの螢、無数にとび立ち、一筋の流れとなり、三宮駅浜側の夏草のしげみに流れおち、くさむら一面無数の螢火にかざられたという、うち捨てられた節子の骨を、守るようにあやすようにあやすように。

That night, countless fireflies flew up from Nunobiki valley and formed a single stream that flowed down into the thicket of weeds outside the bayside exit of Sannomiya Station, covering the area where Setsuko's bones had been thrown away as though to protect and comfort her, comfort her.

The date of Seita's cremation was added to the final paragraph, which focuses in on Seita as one of many nameless war orphans who were cremated en masse and stored in temples as 'abandoned souls'. This paragraph contains two terms that are very rooted in Japanese culture and hard to encapsulate in English: 野垂れ死ぬ (*notarejinu*), which is quite a derogatory term, akin to 'a dog's death', and 無縁仏 (*muenbotoke*), which refers to someone who dies with no living relatives or friends to lay them to rest and pray for their soul, meaning their soul can never rest in peace or attain salvation. Nosaka's use of these terms could be interpreted as emphasizing the futility of Seita's death, and possibly justifying – or at least explaining – his own behaviour. He himself referred to the story as being in the tradition of 心中 (*shinjū*), or lovers' suicide, by which he seemed to mean that the moment Seita took the decision to leave the widow's house and live alone with Setsuko, their fate as outcasts was sealed. While everyone was busy working together trying to survive, and then rebuilding their lives afterwards, Seita and Setsuko cut themselves off and were left behind, denied access to any benefits from society, with no one to look out for them. It's all very well being noble and pure, like Seita, but what's the point when you are doomed to die an ignominious death and never rest in peace?

This new translation of 'Grave of the Fireflies' is being published to commemorate, in September 2025, eighty years since the end of the Second World War, the war that was supposed to end all wars. While working on it, I have been hyper-aware of the fact that, like Seita and Setsuko, many innocent children are still suffering terrible neglect and dying ignominious deaths in numerous conflicts around the world, as well as the fact that we seem to be on the verge of a third world war. I hope it serves as a timely reminder of the grim reality of war, a terrible fate that can befall anyone and should be avoided at all cost. The remaining stories will be translated and released in the first full English translation of Nosaka's original collection in a few years' time.

Ginny Tapley Takemori<br>
September 2025